THE LITTLE TYCOON SERIES

David's First Dollar

written by David Cockey

illustrated by Gau Family Studios

Mom,

Your love, support, and guidance over the years has shaped me from a little boy asking for a dollar to the man I am today. Thank you.

Love,

David

Hi there! I am David and welcome to my world! I live in a nice little town with my mom, dad, and two sisters, Jennifer and Alicia. I am excited for you to join me on my journey as I learn all about money!

On one very hot and steamy summer day, David stared out the window dreaming of the days when he could play outside. It seemed like forever since he last played outside with his sisters and friends. The extreme heat made David feel trapped inside his house.

As David gazed out the window, he heard the faint ringing of an ice cream truck in the distance. As the sweet sound grew louder and the truck drove closer, David ran to his mom and asked, "Please, can I go buy some ice cream from the Ice Cream Man? Please?"

David waited patiently as his mom looked through her purse. Her search seemed to never end. After pulling out credit cards, pens, and her cell phone, disappointed, she looked at her son and said, "David, I am very sorry, but I do not have a dollar for you to get an ice cream cone."

David's smile instantly turned to a frown. His hope for ice cream on this hot summer day disappeared. As David walked away from his mom, he stared out the window at all of the happy children standing around the ice cream truck. All of them had an ice cream cone or a dollar in their hand.

That night, David struggled to fall asleep as ice cream cones and dollars danced in his head. David abruptly sat up in his bed and shouted, "If I had my own dollar, I could buy my own ice cream cone!" Lying back down, David shut his eyes and dreamed of how he could earn his very own dollar.

The next morning, David woke up still thinking about dollars and ice cream. Suddenly, he had an idea!

"I will get a job! That's right! I will get a grown up job like Mom and Dad!" David exclaimed. Although no one was listening, David knew it was a good idea.

David hopped out of bed and rushed to his closet. He searched and hunted for the fancy suit he wore to his Aunt Betsy and Uncle Michael's wedding.

All dressed, he brushed his teeth and slicked back his hair. Before he left his room, he looked in the mirror, winked, and thought, "I am ready to make a dollar!"

David walked into the kitchen where his mom and sisters were eating breakfast. They all turned and looked at him. Pointing and laughing, David's sisters joked about his new look.

Trying to understand her son's new style, David's mom asked, "Where are you going, David?"

"I am going to get a job so I can earn a dollar and buy my very own ice cream cone. Do you think you can help me find a job?" David asked.

"You look so professional and handsome, and I know the perfect place for you to work. You can have a job right here. There is so much work to do and you can help me. I will pay you for each job you complete," David's mother said.

Jennifer and Alicia's laughter fell to silence as the two older sisters looked at each and whispered, "Now that David is working, maybe we can get him to work for us. He can clean our room and do our chores!"

Although David looked very professional in his suit, he was hot and uncomfortable. Almost immediately after he was offered the job to help his mom, he ran upstairs to change his clothes. He was ready to earn his first dollar.

David's first job was to take out all the trash. Most of the trash came from his sisters' room. He wondered, "How can two girls create so much trash?"

After taking out the trash, David anxiously ran to his mom and said, "I am ready for another job."

David's next job was to wash the dishes. David ran into the kitchen, filled up the sink, and washed the dishes from breakfast. One by one, he scrubbed and cleaned each dish, and the number of dishes seemed to never end. David thought, "This is a lot of work! But it will be worth it when I have my dollar and can buy my own ice cream cone!"

After finishing the dishes, David passed by his sisters' room on his way to see what job he would do next. Although Jennifer and Alicia hoped David would clean their room, he was just too busy.

David's next job was to pick up all the toys, clothes, and shoes in the living room and put them where they belonged. After he finished, he thought, "All this work is making me hungry!"

David found his mom and said, "I have built up an
appetite doing all of these jobs. When can we have
lunch?" David knew the ice cream truck usually comes
to his neighborhood after lunch and he needed to earn
his dollar soon.

"Okay David, your last job is to make everyone lunch. Once lunch is done, you will have earned your first dollar." This was David's most difficult job yet, because he did not know what to make and was not known for his skills as a chef.

A light bulb went off and David decided to make everyone his personal favorite, peanut butter and marshmallow sandwiches. He thought to himself, "These sandwiches will not only taste great, but will look great too!"

After lunch, David's mom got her purse to reward him with his first dollar. Much like the day before, she dug through her purse and pulled out a few shiny coins that did not look like dollars. She handed David a quarter for taking out the trash, another quarter for washing the dishes, a quarter for cleaning the living room, and one last quarter for making lunch.

David stared at his hands and the four quarters. Puzzled, he looked up to his Mom and said, "This is not a dollar! These are coins. I need a dollar for my ice cream."

David's mother explained, "You have four quarters and four quarters equals one dollar. Each coin in your hand is worth 25 cents and each dollar is worth 100 cents. Since you have four quarters, you have one dollar. Even though it is not a dollar bill, it is still a dollar and you can use the quarters to buy your ice cream."

David gazed out the window, holding his shiny new dollar in his hand. He was very happy to hear the delightful sound of the ice cream truck.

David could not contain his excitement. When the truck pulled up to the house, he ran as fast as he could through the front door and down the sidewalk to be the first one in line.

"I'll take an ice cream cone!" David ordered from the ice cream man, not realizing he was yelling. He handed the ice cream man the four quarters. After receiving his ice cream, he walked away with a big smile, feeling proud of the hard work he completed to earn his first dollar. David could not remember a better tasting ice cream cone.

As David sat on the curb eating his ice cream, all he could think about was all the money he could earn if he worked tomorrow and the next day and the next. With every lick of the ice cream cone, David thought about how he could make his next dollar.